SCARY TALES RETOLD™

JACK AND THE BLOODY BEANSTALK

by Wiley Blevins • illustrated by Steve Cox

RED CHAIR PRESS

Please visit our website at **www.redchairpress.com** for more high-quality products for young readers.

About the Author

Wiley Blevins has taught elementary school in both the United States and South America. He has also written over 70 books for children and 15 for teachers, as well as created reading programs for schools in the U.S. and Asia with Scholastic, Macmillan/McGraw-Hill, Houghton-Mifflin Harcourt, and other publishers. Wiley currently lives and writes in New York City.

About the Artist

Steve Cox lives in London, England. He first designed toys and packaging for other people's characters. But he decided to create his own characters and turned full time to illustrating. When he is not drawing books he plays lead guitar in a rock band.

Publisher's Cataloging-In-Publication Data

Blevins, Wiley.
    Jack and the bloody beanstalk / by Wiley Blevins ; illustrated by Steve Cox.

    pages : illustrations ; cm. -- (Scary tales retold)

    Summary: "Jack and his poor mother follow all the rules of this classic tale. But can they escape the raging Giant? Jack must return time and again to ask the Giant to return his family's wealth. Each time the Giant makes new demands. Readers will marvel at the twists and turns in this gruesome tale."--Provided by publisher.
    Issued also as an ebook.
    ISBN: 978-1-63440-099-2 (library hardcover)
    ISBN: 978-1-63440-100-5 (paperback)

    1. Boys--Juvenile fiction. 2. Mothers and sons--Juvenile fiction. 3. Giants--Juvenile fiction. 4. Boys--Fiction. 5. Mothers and sons--Fiction. 6. Giants--Fiction. 7. Fairy tales. 8. Horror tales. I. Cox, Steve, 1961- II. Title. III. Title: Based on (work) Jack and the beanstalk.

PZ7.B618652 Ja 2016
[E]   2015940014

Scary Tales Retold first published by:
Red Chair Press LLC   PO Box 333   South Egremont, MA 01258-0333

Printed in the United States of America
Distributed in the U.S. by Lerner Publisher Services. www.lernerbooks.com

0516 1 CBGF16

Long ago and far away, there lived a boy named Jack. He lived with his mother in a tiny hut. They had little money. And almost no food.

"Go and sell our last cow," said Jack's mother. "We need money to buy food for the winter."

So Jack began walking their old cow to the town market.

Along the way, Jack met an odd, little man. "Where are you going?" asked the man. He had an odd, little smile.

"I need to sell my cow," said Jack.

"I have a better idea," said the man.
"I will trade your cow for these
magic beans. Plant them tonight.
By morning they will reach the sky.
Great riches will be yours."

"Wow!" said Jack. "My mother will
be so happy."

"What?" yelled Jack's mother. "You traded our cow for some silly beans. Now we will starve. Off to bed!" And she tossed the beans out the window.

The next morning, Jack looked outside.
A giant beanstalk stretched high into the clouds.

"The man was right," said Jack.
"I must see where this beanstalk goes.
I must find great riches for my mother."

So Jack climbed up and up and up.

At the top of the beanstalk, Jack saw
a house as wide as a town. Around the
house stood large trees with no leaves.
In front of it rested row after row of
gravestones.

"What is this place?" asked Jack.

A thin, ghostly woman glided from behind a tree. "This is a graveyard for those who have angered the giant," she said. "You can find great riches here. But only if the giant doesn't catch you."

"Where is the giant?" asked Jack.

"He's out looking for someone to eat," whispered the thin, ghostly woman. Jack tiptoed into the graveyard. He stopped at a large gravestone.

On it was written . . .

Open this coffin
to find gold in a sack.
But run home fast
before the giant comes back.

Jack slowly lifted the coffin's lid. The coffin was filled with bones. On top of the bones sat a sack of gold. Jack grabbed the sack. As he did, Jack heard loud footsteps.

"Fee, Fi, Fo, Foy.
I smell the blood
Of a tasty little boy."

"The giant is coming back," said the thin, ghostly woman. "Hurry!"

Jack ran as fast as he could. He slid down the beanstalk even faster. The giant's screams filled the air. "Come back and I will eat you in one bite," roared the giant.

Jack handed the sack of gold to his mother.
"This is some of the money the giant stole from
us years ago," she said. "Your father died trying
to get it back. You must go and get the rest.
Take this shield to protect you."

The next morning Jack climbed up the beanstalk. The thin, ghostly woman glided from behind a tree. "You are a brave boy," she whispered. "But beware. The giant is very hungry today."

Jack tiptoed to a gravestone. On it was written his father's name and a message:

*Open this coffin
a surprise lies inside.
All your riches
the giant did hide.*

"My mother will be so happy," said Jack.
He was about to lift the coffin lid when . . .

The giant ran out from the trees.
He grabbed Jack by the legs. The giant lifted
Jack to his mouth.

"Fee, Fi, Fo, Foy.
I am going to eat
A yummy little boy."

Jack screamed. Then he punched the giant
in the nose with his shield. Blood shot out,
pouring down the beanstalk.

The giant screamed and dropped Jack. Then
Jack ran and slid down the bloody beanstalk
until . . .

Jack landed beside his hut. The giant raced
down after him.

Jack grabbed an ax. He chopped and
chopped and chopped. The beanstalk swayed
with each blow.

Jack ran into his hut as the beanstalk and the giant came tumbling down.

THUD!

The giant landed on top of Jack's hut.

That was the end of the giant.
That was the end of Jack and his mother.
And that is the end of this bloody tale.

THE END